Citybook

Written by

Shelley Rotner and Ken Kreisler

Photographs by Shelley Rotner

ORCHARD BOOKS

NEW YORK

Orchard Books
95 Madison Avenue
New York, NY 10016

Manufactured in Singapore

Printed and bound by Toppan Printing Company, Inc.

Book design by Hans Teensma/Impress, Inc.

10 9 8 7 6 5 4 3 2 1

The text of this book is set in Lanston Kaatskill,
designed and produced in Quark XPress on the Macintosh computer.

The illustrations are full-color photographs.

Library of Congress Cataloging-in-Publication Data
Rotner, Shelley.
    Citybook / written by Shelley Rotner and Ken Kreisler ; photographs by Shelley Rotner.
        p. cm.
    Summary: Rhyming text and photographs celebrate the sights and people of the city.
        ISBN 0-531-06837-4   ISBN 0-531-08687-9 (lib. bdg.)
        [1. City and town life—Fiction. 2. Stories in rhyme.]
    I. Kreisler, Ken.   II. Title.   III. Title: City book.
    PZ8.3.R755C1 1994
    [E]--dc20   93-6350

For Stephen
—S.R.

For Shelley
—K.K.

Kevin loved to go to the city.

There was so much to see —

lots of people on the go—

riding buses,

taking taxis,

catching trains,

walking, running, roller blading.

Window shopping,

sometimes stopping.

Mimes, music, museums.

Painted walls

and neon signs.

Long

lines.

Fountains, bridges,

statues,   flags.

So many sights.

So many lights.

City nights.